MAE and JUNE

and the
Wonder Wheel

MAE and JUNE

and the

Wonder Wheel

By Charise Mericle Harper

Illustrated by Ashley Spires

HOUGHTON MIFFLIN HARCOURT

BOSTON   NEW YORK

The text was set in Adobe Garamond Pro.

Library of Congress Cataloging-in-Publication Data
Names: Harper, Charise Mericle, author. | Spires, Ashley, 1978–author.
Title: The Wonder wheel : Mae and June / written by Charise Mericle Harper ;
illustrated by Ashley Spires.
Other titles: Mae and June
Description: Boston : Houghton Mifflin Harcourt, 2017. | Summary: June is
happy to get a new neighbor, Mae, and soon the two of them are best friends and
having adventures determined by the Wonder Wheel that they spin each morning.
Identifiers: LCCN 2015033389 | ISBN 9780544630635 (hardback)
Subjects: | CYAC: Best friends — Fiction. | Play—Fiction. |
Imagination — Fiction. | BISAC: JUVENILE FICTION / Humorous Stories. |
JUVENILE FICTION / Social Issues / Friendship. | JUVENILE FICTION /
Action & Adventure / General. | JUVENILE FICTION / Readers / Chapter
Books. | JUVENILE FICTION / Animals / Pets. | JUVENILE FICTION /
Fantasy & Magic.
Classification: LCC PZ7.H231323 Wo 2017 | DDC [Fic] — dc23 LC record
available at http://lccn.loc.gov/2015033389

Manufactured in the United States of America
DOC 10 9 8 7 6 5 4 3 2 1
4500636822

CHAPTER 1

Sammy is my best friend. He has four legs, really soft ears, and a tail that can wag slow, medium, and super fast. Sometimes it moves so fast it makes his whole bottom shake. When this happens you have to be careful, because a shaking bottom can knock a glass of juice right off a table, but that's not his fault. Tails are hard to control. I like everything about Sammy, but my favorite thing is that he's fun to talk to. I'm lucky. I have the only ears in the whole world that can hear Sammy talk.

Sammy and I have a mission—our first ever. We're looking for a new friend. My sister, Isabella, used to play with us, but now that she's thirteen, she says, *Teenagers don't play baby games.* It's too bad. She's missing out on a lot of fun.

Sammy and I are practicing the three *F*s. We bounce on my bed and shout them out loud.

"FUN! FRIENDLY! FULL OF ADVENTURE!"

They are important, because our new friend must ABSOLUTELY and DEFINITELY be all three.

After five times in a row, Sammy jumps down and runs to the door. "Last one to the kitchen is a rotten egg!"

I'm always the rotten egg, but I don't care. It's not fair racing. Sammy has more legs than me.

When I get to the kitchen, Sammy smiles and holds up his foot. "Power Paws win!"

I stomp my feet like I'm mad, but I'm only acting. "June Feet lose!"

"UGH!" complains Isabella. "Do you always have to pretend-talk to the dog? It's embarrassing." She waves her hand. "Go play outside."

"PLAY!" shouts Sammy, and he runs to the back door.

As soon as we're outside, I show him my pocket.

"Chocolate chip cookies!" His tail wags extra fast.

I pull one out, break off the chocolate chips, and pop them into my mouth. Chocolate can poison a dog, so I have to eat them. I only give Sammy the cookie part.

"CHOCOLATE!" cries Sammy, and he drops to the ground and plays dead.

I fall down next to him, and then we roll and howl like zombies.

CHAPTER 2

We have new neighbors. A girl, a teenage boy, a mom, a dad, and a cat are all moving into the house across the street.

Mom wants me to go over and meet the new girl, but I say, "No thank you. I'll wait for the lemon cake."

Next Saturday she's going to make two of them: one to keep, and one to give to the new neighbors. That's a smart way to make people like you. Bring them something delicious.

The only person not happy with the plan is

Isabella. "Why do I have to go? I'll die of embarrassment!"

Dad is not worried about her dying. "Five minutes of friendly chatting is not going to kill you."

"But I don't talk to boys!" screams Isabella, and then she stomps off.

Sammy and I go up to my room. Staying away from Isabella is a good idea.

My window is perfect for spying on the house across the street. The new girl's outside, hopping on one foot.

"Maybe she can be our new friend," says Sammy.

I'm thinking that too. I say the three *F*s out loud. "Fun. Friendly. Full of Adventure."

"Do you think she has them?" asks Sammy.

We watch, but it's hard to tell if she has the three *F*s just by looking.

When she runs up and down the moving truck ramp I say, "That looks like fun."

Sammy shakes his head. "Or a bee could be chasing her."

When she waves goodbye to the moving truck people, I say, "That looks friendly."

Sammy shakes his head again. "Maybe the bee came back."

When she digs a hole in the ground, Sammy gets super excited. "I bet she's hunting for dinosaur bones."

I'm excited too. "Digging looks adventurous!"

But then her dad comes out and plants a mini flagpole. The

flag looks nice, but a flower flag is not the kind of flag that is full of adventure.

"Rumble tummy," moans Sammy.

I know what he means. I'm hungry too. We go to the kitchen, but before we get there, I make him promise that after lunch we'll watch some more.

CHAPTER 3

Spying is not always fun. Sammy and I are looking out the window, but all we see is a house. No one's outside. Nothing is happening.

Sammy's not usually a complainer, but today he's an expert at it. "What if she never comes out? She's been inside forever! Are we going to do this all day?" He puts his head down on the window ledge and sighs super loud.

His complaining is reminding me of someone else. Someone named April.

April sits across the table from me at school.

She acts like she's queen of the world, but really she's queen of two other things — complaining and talking about herself. Listening to her all day is torture, but Mrs. Warble, my teacher, won't let me change seats.

When I asked, she shook her head and said, "Imagine the rainbow. It needs every color to be beautiful."

I know all the rainbow colors by heart. It's easy, if you remember ROY G BIV (red, orange, yellow, green, blue, indigo, violet). If people were colors, April would be indigo! Indigo is bossy. Indigo could cover up every other color and not let them even peek through a little bit. I imagine a new rainbow without indigo. Mrs. Warble is wrong. ROY G BV would still be beautiful.

"LOOK!" Sammy puts his paws up on the window. "She's back!"

I look up. The new girl is on her front porch. She checks her shoelaces, pushes the doorbell, and then takes off running.

"A JOGGER!" shouts Sammy. His tail wags. Sammy loves running, but instead of jogging on the sidewalk, the girl runs across the lawn, jumps over some bushes, and disappears behind the house. A few seconds later, she comes running back from around the other side. She's running around her whole house. But why? It's a good question, and I wish I knew the answer. At the front door, the girl pushes the doorbell and goes inside.

Sammy nudges my hand. "That counts as fun!" But then a second later he shakes his head. "Or it could have been the bee chasing her again."

CHAPTER

Sammy and I are taking a break from spying. We're playing On-the-Ground Disco Dancing. It's like regular dancing, only you do it lying down. Sammy and I have a great new routine. We can dance and point in all different directions at the same time. The music is about to start.

Sammy is the leader. "Paw up!"

I don't have a paw, so I hold up my hand.

He counts down. "Five, four, three, two . . ." And then the doorbell rings.

The music starts, but suddenly I'm all alone.

Sammy's gone, barking and racing for the front door. I jump up and chase after him. I catch up just as Mom opens the door.

She points to Sammy. "DO SOMETHING WITH HIM!"

I lean down next to Sammy's ear. "Great barking, but can you keep the rest inside?"

It's not easy to stop doing something you love, but Sammy tries. He closes his mouth and puts his head down. His barks still want to come out, but he keeps his teeth so tight together that only a little growl escapes. I scratch behind his ears. That helps him keep calm.

Mom is talking to Mr. Robertson from

next door. When he leaves, there's a giant box on the porch. Mom points to the name on top —*June Fairway.* That's ME!

Isabella's full of questions. "What is it? Who's it for? Who sent it?"

I know two of the answers. "It's a present to me from Mr. Robertson."

Isabella doesn't believe me. "Mr. Robertson from next door gave *you* a present?"

Mom laughs and shakes her head. "No, it's not from Mr. Robertson. We were out yesterday when the box was delivered. Mr. Robertson was just saving it for us."

Isabella pokes it with her foot. "What's inside?"

Sammy jumps up. He has a great idea. "LET'S MAKE GUESSES!"

While Mom and Isabella pull the box into

the house, Sammy and I dance around the room and shout out guesses.

"Cupcakes! Porcupines! Chocolate! Candy!"

"Dinosaur bones! Squirrels! Bones! Squirrels!"

"IT'S FROM GRANDMA PENNY!" Mom waves a piece of paper in the air.

I stop dancing. A present from Grandma Penny is worth stopping for, because Grandma Penny is absolutely the best present giver in the whole world.

CHAPTER

Grandma Penny lives far away. That's the sad part, but the not sad part is that when she does visit, it's fun, fun, fun all the time.

After her visits, Mom always says the same thing. "That Grandma Penny sure is a free spirit."

Then Dad says, "You can say that again."

So Mom laughs and says it again. Being a double free spirit is the biggest compliment a person can get. It means they are not even one percent boring.

Mom pats the box. "I'll get some scissors."

While she's gone, Sammy and I talk about free spirits.

"Am I one?" asks Sammy.

I shake my head. Sometimes Sammy takes too many naps, and barking at squirrels is only fun for the first five minutes.

Sammy shrugs. "That's okay, two double free spirits is probably too much for one family."

I know he's only teasing, because I am definitely a double free spirit.

"Uh-oh!" Sammy points behind me.

I spin around. Isabella is pulling a long piece of tape off the box. She's opening MY PRESENT! I yell at her, but she doesn't look up, so I yell again and jump in front of her.

She looks surprised. "Oh, I thought you were talking to the dog."

I'm glad when Mom gets back. She cuts the tape with her scissors, and makes Isabella keep her hands to herself.

Now Isabella's grumpy. "I was only helping. A thank-you would be nice."

I ignore her, open the flaps, and look inside. Sammy nudges me. "What is it?"

I'm not sure what to call it, so I describe it instead. "It's round and pointy."

"PORCUPINE!" shouts Sammy. "Hold it up!"

I shake my head. It's not a porcupine, and it's too heavy for me to lift up.

I let Mom and Isabella pull the present out. There are two pieces; a big flat wheel with pegs all around the edge of it, and a stand with a long pole that sticks straight up in the air.

Mom is smiling. "It's a spinning wheel, like on *Wheel of Fortune.*"

"The TV show?" asks Isabella.

"Exactly," says Mom. "Let's put it together."

CHAPTER 6

A spinning wheel put together is a lot more exciting than a spinning wheel in pieces. It looks perfect next to my dresser.

Isabella throws a plastic bag full of chalk onto my bed. "It came with the wheel."

I look over. The front of the wheel is black like a chalkboard.

Mom claps her hands. "It's a perfect family chore wheel. There can be a space for doing the dishes, setting the table, folding the laundry . . ."

"NO!" Isabella and I both shout at the same

time. Everyone laughs. I'm glad Mom's only joking. A chore wheel is a terrible present.

Mom checks the wheel then gives me a thumbs-up. I grab the side and pull down. Suddenly it's spinning. *Tackity, tackity, tackity*— a rubber flipper at the top of the pole hits the pegs as they go by.

Sammy's tail is wagging. He smiles at the wheel. "It sounds like a hundred WOOD-PECKERS!" Woodpeckers are his favorite bird.

"It'll spin forever," groans Isabella. Mom said she can have a turn when it stops. She plops down on my bed and studies her nails. Isabella's the queen of nail polish. Today she has polka dots. Maybe she's counting them.

When the wheel stops, Isabella's ready. She pulls down hard. Now it sounds like a thousand woodpeckers. Sammy and I spin in circles, then

fall down laughing and dizzy. Isabella rolls her eyes. She's good at spinning eyeballs.

As soon as the wheel slows down, Sammy jumps up. He wants us to guess. When will it stop?

He guesses first. "Eighteen tackitys!"

I guess fifteen.

We're both wrong—it's twenty-two, but we jump and cheer anyway. Isabella shakes her head and walks toward the door. She doesn't say a word. Not even goodbye, or thank you.

Sammy looks at me. "I bet she guessed wrong too. Not everyone's a good loser."

When I look back, Isabella's gone and Mom's walking in.

She holds up a big yellow envelope. "Look what I found taped inside the box."

It's heavy, too heavy to be just a card. On the back are six important words: *For June and Sammy's eyes only.*

CHAPTER 7

Sammy's name has never been on an envelope before. He can't wait to see inside. He's excited and panting and close — too close! He drools on my hand. YUCK! I wipe it off on my pants.

"Five, four, three, two, one." I open the envelope and turn it upside down.

A piece of white paper wrapped around more yellow envelopes falls out.

"Is that it?" Sammy jumps off the bed and looks around, but there's nothing else. I pull off

the paper. It's a note from Grandma Penny. I
start reading.

> Dear June and Sammy, I hope you like
> your new Wonder Wheel.

"IT'S A WONDER WHEEL!" shouts
Sammy.

Wonder Wheel is a good
name. Now I like
it even more.

Sammy pokes the note with his nose. "What's next?"

Now there's a wet spot on the paper, but I don't say anything. I just keep reading.

I have included six yellow envelopes for you. You can open a new one every Monday morning. Inside you will find instructions on how to set up the Wonder Wheel for the week. Remember, this is not a magic wheel. It only invites you to wonder and to see how little things can change your life. Have fun! I can't wait to hear about your adventures. Love, Grandma Penny.

"Let's start!" Sammy hops off the bed.

I'm excited too, but I want to follow the

rules. Today is Sunday, not Monday. We have to wait.

Sammy points to the envelopes. "Can we pick one out if we don't open it?"

That's a great idea, and doing something is always better than doing nothing. I let Sammy pick. He studies the envelopes, then pulls one out with his paw. I put it on the dresser. We both stare at it. Sammy's like me. Wondering what's inside.

I point to the wheel. "Setting up might take a while. We should get up early."

Sammy looks up. "How early?"

I hold up four fingers and two thumbs. That makes six in the morning.

He shakes his head. "I was hoping for earlier."

I know what he means. It's hard to wait. I give the wheel a spin, just for fun.

"Woodpeckers," says Sammy, and he closes his eyes.

CHAPTER 8

Sammy and I wake up before the alarm clock. That kind of thing only happens when we're super excited. Sammy jumps off the bed and gets the envelope. I open it. Inside is a folded-up note and another envelope. The note says *READ ME FIRST* and the envelope says *WORD GUIDE*.

"Read READ ME FIRST!" whispers Sammy. That sounds funny—I almost laugh out loud, but then I stop myself. We definitely and absolutely can't make any noise. If Isabella wakes up before

her normal time, we're in trouble. She's scary in the mornings.

I open the note and read it to Sammy.

WONDER WHEEL INSTRUCTIONS

Number one—Use your chalk to divide the wheel into six slices.

There's a picture of a circle with three lines on it. I've never thought about it before, but three lines makes six slices.

Sammy licks his lips. "It looks like a pizza! Let's have pizza for breakfast."

I shake my head. "It's pancake day." He licks again. Mom always makes him one too. I point to the note. There's a lot to read.

Number two—Here are the words for each slice. Write them on the wheel.

  1. Questions
  2. Animal
  3. Dance/Spin Again
  4. Hand
  5. Poem
  6. Collection

Number three—Spin the wheel. The rubber flipper will stop on a slice with a word in it. Go to the Word Guide envelope. Inside you will find a note with that word on it. These will be your instructions for the day.

Number four—Each day before you spin, be sure to erase the word that you landed on the day before. And also erase one of the lines on the side of that slice. This way your empty slice will join another slice. Don't worry, some slices will be bigger than others.

Number five—Spin and erase every day until you're done.

Exception—Dance/Spin Again never gets erased.

Sammy runs over to the wheel. I pick out a piece of chalk and follow him. His tail's wagging super fast. If I had a tail, it would be wagging like crazy too.

CHAPTER 9

It takes a while to set up the wheel. It's not easy to draw a straight line on a wheel that moves, and Sammy wants every slice to be exactly even. He whispers out comments—*too squiggly, too skinny, too chunky, too curvy.* These are not the kind of words that make a person feel good about their drawing, but when I'm finally done he says, "Perfect." And I feel better. Writing the words is easier and faster. I step back to look. The Wonder Wheel is beautiful.

"Spin it!" says Sammy.

I grab the wheel and pull down. We dance to the tackitys, until the wheel slows down, and then we stop and watch. This is the

important part. Which slice will win? *Tackity, tackity, tack.* It's ANIMAL!

Sammy spins in a circle. "I pick squirrels. They're fun to chase."

I look through the Word Guide envelope, find the animal note, and read it.

ANIMAL

Pick an animal you admire. This will be your spirit animal for the day. Today you will try to act like your animal.

Example: If you picked lion, you will try to be fierce and brave.

Remember, use your animal to help you. Think . . . What would a <u>your animal name here</u> do?

PS. You do not have to walk like, talk like, or eat the favorite food of your animal. Have fun!

Sammy nudges my arm. "Can I be your spirit animal?"

I rub his ears. "What about squirrels?"

Sammy shakes his head. "Admire and fun to chase are different things. Admire is a lot more important."

I hug Sammy and whisper in his ear. "Okay, it's you!"

Sammy bounces on the bed while I look in

my closet. A special day needs a special outfit. When I'm done, I have on my I LOVE DOGS sweatshirt, a pair of dog knee socks, a dancing dog skirt, and my dog heart jewelry. That's a lot of dog stuff to wear at once. Sammy gives me a paws-up and barks three times. That's his I-like-it bark. It's a big compliment.

CHAPTER 10

Not everyone likes my outfit as much as Sammy. As soon as I walk into the kitchen, Isabella scrunches up her nose.

"You're wearing that?"

I get ready for more questions, but she doesn't ask any—her mouth's too full of pancake. Isabella's a big complainer on Monday mornings. She doesn't like going back to school, but Mom is smart. She knows that a full mouth is a quiet mouth. Sammy's pancake is gone in two seconds. It's bad planning, because now he has to watch

me eat mine, and I don't share pancakes, even if
he drools.

After breakfast I get ready for school, then
give Sammy an extra-big hug before I leave. He
watches me from the living room window and I

wave from the sidewalk. Suddenly he's barking. Why? I look around, and then I see what he sees. The new girl's across the street, with her dad, walking in the same direction as me. She's going to my school!

At the corner, I speed up and cross the street. Then, I sneak up on them, just like Sammy does with squirrels. Now I can hear what they're saying. The new girl's nervous.

Her dad holds her hand. "It's okay. You'll find a new friend."

I smile. The new friend might be me.

For the whole rest of the way, they are quiet. As soon as we get to the playground, the bell rings and I have to run past them. If you're in Mrs. Warble's class, you do not want to be late.

Olivia is standing at Mrs. Warble's desk, but that's not unusual. She gets into trouble a lot, and usually it's for arguing with Steven, her twin brother. They are not the kind of twins that are alike. Olivia is bossy and smart and Steven is not those things, except he could be smart, but it's hard to tell, because he likes making up bad jokes more than he likes giving right answers. I look for Steven. He's in his seat, smiling. When one of them is in trouble, the other one's always super happy.

CHAPTER 11

I sit down and take out my books, but then I feel something. Eyes are like that—sometimes you can feel them working, even if they belong to someone else. I look up. April is staring straight at me. She points to her shirt. It has kittens on it. They're cute. I smile. She leans forward to talk. Maybe she likes my shirt too.

She points and sneers. "Cats are better than dogs."

My brain's surprised. Too surprised to make words.

Suddenly someone's next to me, leaning on my desk. "No way! Dogs are better!"

It's Steven, from two seats over. Where's Jennifer? She's supposed to sit in between us.

Steven holds up his hand. "High-five for dogs!"

I look back at April. She's smiling her I'm-so-smart smile. I don't like that smile. It makes me feel like a volcano. A volcano that wants to

explode! I high-five Steven's hand, and then I growl, just like Sammy does when he's mad.

"GRRRR!" Steven growls too.

April looks surprised, but then she flips her hair and ignores us. She opens her pencil case and takes out her pencils. She has a collection.

I cover my mouth. I can't believe it! I just growled at April. That spirit animal stuff is a lot stronger than I thought it would be. And then a few minutes later, everyone in the whole class is talking about cats and dogs!

Mrs. Warble surprises us. Instead of getting mad she says, "Charts can help with math. Let's make a pet popularity chart."

"Petularity chart," says Steven.

He thinks that's funny, putting words together. He's wrong.

When we're done, there are fifteen *X*s in the

cat column, eleven *X*s in the dog column, and one *X* in the rabbit column—Olivia likes to be different.

April is smiling. I know why. She's happy that the cat side has more *X*s. I decide not to look at her for the whole rest of the day, but then I have to, because suddenly she's shouting.

"LOOK! Another *X*!" She points to the door.

Mr. Flint, our principal, is walking in, but he's not the *X*. It's the girl next to him. The new girl, and right on the front of her shirt is a smiling cat.

CHAPTER 12

Mrs. Warble puts the new girl in the empty seat next to me. Her name is Mae. Now I'm glad that Jennifer's away. This is the perfect way for us to become friends. I sneak a peek. Mae looks nervous. I need to say the exact right thing to make her feel better. But before I can think of it, April starts talking to her.

"Cats are the cutest. Look!" She holds out her shirt. "Plus, guess what? I'm April. Get it? April and Mae."

Mae smiles. April grins and points.

"You can have lunch with me and Ava. That's her over there. We have a cat club."

Ava waves from the table behind April. She's April's best friend. They do everything together. Mae waves back.

What is she talking about? "CAT CLUB! WHAT CAT CLUB?" I only mean to think the words, but by accident, my mouth says them out loud. Now Mae is looking at me.

I smile. "I'm June."

Mae looks back and forth, like she can't believe it. "April, Mae, and June?"

April glares at me. "Forget June—she's in the dog club."

"Dog club rules!" Steven high-fives the air, but then pulls down his arm and rubs it, an eraser bouncing off his desk onto the floor. Olivia snort-laughs from the table behind us. She scored a perfect hit, right in the arm. Steven scrunches up a piece of paper and throws it. Olivia yelps. I know what's coming next. TROUBLE!

April shakes her head. "Dog people are crazy. Here." She rolls a pencil across the table to Mae. "It's from my collection. You can have it."

Mae picks it up, smiles, and says thank you. I can tell already. She likes April.

Mrs. Warble stomps past us. She has triangle arms. That's how you can tell if she's mad. She takes Steven and Olivia out into the hallway. No one's surprised.

I want to say something to Mae — something that will make her like me. I think of my spirit

animal. What would Sammy do? But instead of an answer, I just feel like a sad dog. I look down at my desk. If I had a tail, it would definitely not be wagging.

CHAPTER 13

April always sits at the end of the lunch table.
Today, Mae's there too. I can't hear what they're
saying, but they're laughing and smiling. Are
they talking about cats? Are they making fun of
dogs?

I'm sitting next to Leni and Jules. We eat
together, and play together at recess, but we're
not the kind of friends who go to each other's
houses.

"Why . . ." asks Jules. And then she takes a

giant bite of her sandwich. Now we have to wait until she's done chewing to find out more.

Jules swallows and points at me. ". . . are you wearing so much dog stuff?"

"Oh." Leni waves her hand. "Is it okay that I'm a cat person?"

I nod. "I like cats."

"Really?" Leni's surprised. "But you look so doggy."

Now I'm embarrassed. Does everyone think I look strange? Dog day is harder than I thought it would be. What would a dog do? Run away? Hide? And then I think about Sammy. Sammy would not run off. Sammy would be excited. Sammy would shout, "YAY FOR DOG DAY!" And then he'd bounce around the room and his energy would make everyone love Dog Day as much as him.

I look around. I'm not going to shout and bounce in the lunchroom. Can I be like Sammy from here? From my chair?

I count to five and then do it. "Today's dog day. I made up a day, for my dog. For fun!"

Jules and Leni are quiet, and then Leni nods. "I get it. That is kind of fun."

Jules slams her hands on the table. She's smiling. "What if we make up a day too! Tomorrow can be . . ."

"CRAZY HAIR DAY!" shouts Leni.

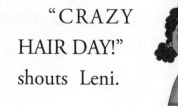

"We can wear crazy hairstyles!" She fluffs her hair.

And then we are talking and laughing so much, that I almost forget about April and Mae. When I sneak a look, they are watching us, but only Mae is smiling.

"We'll spread the word at recess!" shouts Jules.

Leni's super excited. "Everyone will want to do it!"

I smile and nod, but I'm not so sure about the everyone part.

CHAPTER

14

When I get home, Sammy and I roll around on the floor and I tell him about my day.

He's surprised about Mae—"WOW! You got to meet her!"

Now he's extra excited. He jumps up and runs down the hall. I pull off my sock, roll it into a ball, and throw it. He catches it and brings it back. While we play, he asks me questions I can't answer.

"Does Mae have the three *F*s? Does Mae like bones? Does Mae like dogs?"

I shrug and he looks disappointed. I am too. I'll try harder tomorrow.

I save the best news for last, when we're bouncing on my bed. "Guess what?"

Sammy tries, but all of his guesses are about bones, so finally I just tell him.

"Because of be-like-a-dog day, my friends invented crazy hair day!"

"CRAZY HAIR DAY!" shouts Sammy, and he bounces extra high. We bounce and shout a hundred times and then stop. Resting feels good.

Sammy has a question. "What's crazy hair day?"

I hold up my hair. "A day for funny hairstyles."

Sammy nods. "That's not as fun, but probably safer than hair going crazy."

I try to imagine Sammy's thinking. It's funny, but scary, too.

At dinner, I tell everyone about the wheel, and dog day, and crazy hair day.

"That Grandma Penny," says Mom.

"She's full of ideas," says Dad.

Isabella shakes her head. "I'm glad I didn't get a wheel. Being me is hard enough. I don't need extra projects."

After dinner, Isabella comes to my room. She stands in the doorway. "Do you want me to do your hair for you?"

I'm surprised. That sounds exactly like an

extra project. But I don't say anything. I just nod.

Isabella points to my clock. "You'll have to get up early. Crazy hair takes longer than regular hair."

I want to jump and twirl, but instead I only say thank you. Teenagers are tricky. Too much happiness could make her change her mind.

CHAPTER
15

Sammy wakes me up. He's filled with energy. He spins in a circle four times then runs to the wheel. "Woodpeckers! Spin it fast!"

I pull down. I'm still tired. Tack-ity. Tack-ity. Tack-ity. It's a slow spin. A minute later the wheel stops, right on QUESTIONS.

I find the note and read it.

QUESTIONS

Asking questions is a good way to get to know

people and make them feel good. Pick three people who are not family members or close friends. Ask them these two questions.

What is the best thing that has happened to you this week?

What is the worst thing that has happened to you this week?

Have fun!

Picking my own best and worst is easy. My best is meeting Mae and my worst is April being friends with her. That's not a fun thing to think about first thing in the morning.

"LET'S GO!"

The words surprise me. It's Isabella.

When we get to her room, she points to her chair. "SIT!"

Isabella's bossy, even first thing in the morning. Sammy and I both sit—me in the chair and Sammy on the floor. Dogs aren't allowed on her bed.

Isabella brushes my hair. "How about a crazy *cute* hairstyle, instead of just a crazy one?"

I nod.

"Keep still." She pokes me with the brush.

It's hard to sit and do nothing, so I tell her about Mae.

Isabella talks too. "I've seen the brother. He's in my French class. His name's Rocket."

66

I want to ask questions, but I can't open my mouth. She's spraying my head with hair spray and it tastes terrible. I close my eyes and hold my breath.

She pokes me again. "Done."

When I open my eyes, she's holding a mirror. I look. There are two little triangle braids right on the top of my head. They look like ears.

"Squirrel ears," says Isabella. She points the hairbrush at Sammy. "For you and your friend."

"SQUIRRELS?" Sammy runs to the window.

I love my hair! And then I do something I can't help. I give Isabella a giant hug. And, SURPRISE! She hugs me back.

CHAPTER

16

I run all the way to school. I want to see Mae's hair and ask her the Wonder Wheel questions. Jules is waiting for me in the playground. She has braids—eight of them. When she shakes her head, they swing up into the air like octopus legs. She likes my hair even after I tell her they aren't cat ears.

Jules shakes her head. "Cat ears and squirrel ears kind of look the same."

When we get to class, Mae is standing at Mrs. Warble's desk. She has a giant circle braid on the very top of her head. I go over to talk to her, but Mrs. Warble stops me.

She points to my table, "June, your seat, please."

And then I see Jennifer. She's back and sitting in her chair! Now Mae can't be next to me anymore. I slump in my seat. This day is not staying happy.

Jennifer's sad too. "I didn't know about crazy hair day. I didn't get to do it."

I look across at April. Her hairstyle is almost the same as Mae's. The only difference is, April has a bird right in the middle of her braid. It makes it look like a nest. Does Mae have a bird? Did I miss it? I turn to look, but someone pokes me in the arm. It's Steven.

"Why do you have cat ears?"

"I don't. They're squirrel ears!"

He's leaning in front of Jennifer. She looks squished and mad. She grunts and pushes him away. I know what comes next—TROUBLE! Steven likes trouble, so before he can do anything, I ask him the Wonder Wheel questions.

"What's the best and worst thing that happened to you this week?"

He's surprised. For a second he glares at Jennifer, but then he shakes his head and answers.

"The best is that my parents said we could get a pet, and the worst is that it can't be a dog and Olivia wants a rabbit."

"RABBITS!" squeals Jennifer. "I have one!" And then she tells us how it poops in a litterbox and can play fetch with a toy carrot.

"Rabbitastic!" says Steven.

It's a bad joke, but when Jennifer smiles, I smile too.

CHAPTER

17

Mae has a new seat at the front of the class. All I can see is the back of her head. This is not going to help us become friends. When the lunch bell rings, she's waiting by the door.

She smiles. "Nice cat ears."

I shake my head. "They're squirrel ears."

"SQUIRREL EARS!" She bounces on her toes. "I *love* squirrels. That's even my cat's name!"

A cat named Squirrel? Sammy's not going to believe it.

Mae pats the top of her head. "My hair's not finished. I still need a bird. I was going to use my lucky blue bird, but I lost him when we moved."

Losing things is never good, but then I have an idea. "What about a paper bird? You could draw one, color it, and cut it out."

Mae smiles. "Great idea!"

I want to say, *I can help too,* but April is suddenly next to us.

She scowls at me, then turns to Mae. "I can't wait to come over tomorrow and meet your cat."

Mae nods. "It'll be fun." She points to her desk. "I need some stuff to make a bird."

After she's gone, April and I just stand there waiting. It's uncomfortable. Someone should say something. All I can think of is the Wonder

Wheel questions. I'm sure April won't answer them. She'll probably just ignore me, but I'm feeling brave, so I ask anyway.

"What's the best and worst thing that happened to you this week?"

She looks surprised, but then a minute later, she surprises me. She answers.

"The best is meeting Mae, and the worst is you growling at me and trying to steal my friend!"

 I feel bad about the growling, but she's wrong about the stealing. I try to explain. I tell her I saw Mae first, but she holds up her hand.

"STOP TALKING!"

Then she takes a step closer. "Mae sits with me at lunch! I'm going to her house! She's my friend, not yours! STOP BEING A FRIEND STEALER!"

April turns and stomps into the class to find Mae. I don't watch. I feel sick. And even though I'm not even one bit hungry, my feet move toward the lunchroom.

CHAPTER

18

I can't eat lunch, and even after recess, I still feel bad. For the whole afternoon, I don't look over at April or Mae, not once. When the bell rings, I grab my stuff and run. Today's park day, and Mom and Sammy are waiting for me at the school gate. I give them giant hugs.

Mom sees my sad feelings right away. "June, what's wrong?"

I tell her everything.

She hugs me tight. "You

aren't a friend stealer. You and April need to let Mae pick her own friends. Maybe she wants you all to be friends together?"

Being friends with April is not something I've thought about. I'm not sure I can do it, but knowing I'm not a friend stealer makes me feel better.

Sammy and I both love the park. He loves chasing squirrels, and I love the big round swing. Today someone's already on the swing. I can't believe it. It's Mae! Is April here too? I look around but don't see her.

Mom points to the swing. "Looks like fun."

I nod, but I can't stop thinking about April. What if she's right? What if Mae only wants to be friends with her?

I let Sammy off the leash. "Let's chase squirrels."

"SQUIRRELS!" shouts Sammy, and I race after him.

Sammy never gets tired, but I need a rest and a drink, so I stop at the water fountain. The water is warm, but it's better than nothing. When I finish, Mae is standing right in front of me.

"Want to walk to school tomorrow?"

It's a surprise question, but I know the answer. I smile and nod like crazy. Now's the perfect time. I ask her the Wonder Wheel questions.

CHAPTER

19

Today's my lucky day. I'm walking to school with Mae. I like my new rhyme. I say it in my head, over and over, maybe a hundred times.

Sammy's excited too. "We've got one *F* checked and only two more to go! An invitation to walk definitely counts as Friendly." He points his paw. "Don't forget to look for the other two, Fun and Full of Adventure."

I nod, but I know something already. I want Mae to be my friend, no matter what.

Mae doesn't have to think about it. She answers right away. "Making new friends is the best, and losing my lucky blue bird is the worst."

"Is that what he looks like?" I point to the blue paper bird with big yellow eyes peeking out from her braid.

She nods and gives him a pat.

"JUNE! Time to go!" It's Mom calling me.

I smile at Mae. "See you tomorrow!" And then I turn and run.

I spin the wheel and we dance to the tackitys. I could dance all day. I cross my fingers and hope for Dance/Spin Again, but the crossing doesn't work. Collection is the winner.

COLLECTION

Pick a color. Today you will have a scavenger hunt to find seven things of that color. Scraps of paper, bottle tops, leaves—anything found can be part of your collection.

You can ask friends to help too. Happy collecting! Have fun!

Sammy wags his tail. "BLUE!"
It's a good choice.

When I get to the kitchen, I tell Mom about the collection. She finds me a bag. It's plastic and the kind we use for leftovers.

"Blue garbage, how fancy," jokes Isabella. She's in a good mood. Today's band practice and she loves music. Her clarinet's in a special little suitcase right next to her chair. I'm not allowed to touch it.

A little suitcase would be a good place to keep a collection.

I ask Mom if she has one, but she says, "Be happy with what you have."

That means no.

After breakfast I race to get ready. I get outside just as Mae's crossing the street. We wave at Sammy in the window.

On the way to school, I tell her about the Wonder Wheel and the collection, and then we look for blue things. It's not easy. We only find one small broken piece of blue plastic. I put it in the bag.

Mae shakes her head. "Brown would be easier."

I look around. She's right. The world is filled with brown things.

"Do you want this?" She points to the blue elastic ponytail holder in her hair.

I shake my head, but I'm happy she offered. It's the kind of thing a friend would do.

CHAPTER 20

Finding blue things in the classroom is easier. I find a blue eraser, a blue cardboard circle, and a blue pen cap. Mae sits with April at lunchtime, but I'm not sad. We got to walk to school together.

"You can sit with us too," says Mae, but after one look at April I say, "No thank you." It's not easy to swallow food when someone is glaring at you. April's not like me. She doesn't like sharing.

I sit with Jules and Leni, and when Mae sees me looking at her, she smiles and waves. April looks grumpy, but I don't care. I wave back. Jules and Leni want to hear all about my collection, and then they want to help.

"Only seven things?" Jules shakes her head. "I bet we find a hundred."

When the bell rings, we race out to the playground. Finding small blue things is not as easy as we thought it would be. We find a lot of blue things, but shirts, jackets, hats, and lunchboxes are too big. And then Jules finds the best thing so far — a little blue plastic owl.

"It looks like part of a game or something." She cleans it off with water from her water bottle. We pass it around. It's smooth and nice to hold.

Leni invents a new game. It's like regular tag, except you have tag people with the blue owl, and you can throw it, but only at their feet. Nobody wants a blue owl in the eye. Mae plays too.

It's one of our best recesses ever.

When we get back to class, I take out my collection bag, just to look. Jennifer and Steven are talking about rabbits, but then Jennifer puts her hand out and drops a blue rubber band right in front of me. She points to Steven. "It's from him."

Steven nods.

I'm surprised, but happy. I whisper back a thank-you. Now I have six things—only one more blue thing to go.

CHAPTER 21

It's no fun walking home. All I can think about is April and Mae and their playdate. It's not the same as lunchtime. Sharing is not easy.

April and Mae. Mae and June. Which sounds better? I almost forget to look for blue things, but then the sun shines right on a blue bottle cap in the grass. Seven things. The collection is done, but I'm not excited. It doesn't feel like I thought it would.

When I get to my house, I look across the street, no one's outside at Mae's house. I can't decide if that's good or bad. Are they having fun inside? I turn and walk to my door, and then I see it—a bright blue circle, right on my top front step. It's Mae's ponytail holder. Grandma Penny was

wrong. Eight is the perfect number for a happy collection!

Sammy is happy to see me. After a snack, and a chasing game, we go upstairs.

He's worried. "Are you sure you want to look?"

I nod. "I have to."

We get to the window just in time. Mae is running around her house, just like before, but this time she's holding something.

I point. "That's April, by the front door."

Sammy snorts. He doesn't like her either.

When Mae gets back to the front door, she hands April what she's holding and then April starts running.

It looks like a relay race!

April runs across the yard and disappears behind the house just like Mae did, but she's not as fast as Mae. It's taking her a long time to come back.

Sammy shakes his head. "I bet she got lost."

Mae must be worried, because she leaves the steps and runs off behind the house.

Sammy sees them first. "Look! She found her. They're coming!"

We watch them walk up to the door and go inside.

"Relay race?" asks Sammy. "Does that count as an *F* for Full of Adventure?"

I nod, and then I tell him about owl tag at recess. "That was definitely fun!"

"THE THREE *F*s!" shouts Sammy. "It's official! She did it!" He bounces on the bed.

I'm happy too, but not for the three *F*s. They don't really matter anymore. Mae's already my friend.

CHAPTER 22

There are only three slices left on the Wonder Wheel—POEM, HAND and DANCE/SPIN AGAIN—but still it's exciting.

We watch until it stops.

"Hand!" I shout out. "PEOPLE PAW!" shouts Sammy. We high-five.

I read out the instructions.

HAND.

Today you will give out a helping hand. Trace

your hand onto a piece of paper, then cut out the hand shape. A helping hand can be a promise to help with something, or information that might be helpful. Write it on the hand. Have fun!

I make a helping hand for me, and then a helping paw for Sammy.

He's excited about his extra paw. He says he's going to keep it forever.

At breakfast, Isabella has a big announcement. "I'm trying out to be in a rock band. The audition's tomorrow."

Mom's surprised. "With the clarinet?"

Isabella nods. "I probably won't be good enough."

"Nonsense!" says Mom. "You play beautifully."

I'm not sure that *rock band* and *play beautifully* go together, but Isabella likes the compliment.

Mae and I are walking to school again. She's waiting for me on the sidewalk when I get outside. I smile, but she doesn't smile back.

"Oh, June, it's terrible. April's going to be mad at me forever."

And then she tells me why.

"We were having a race, running around the house with an egg on a spoon, but then April dropped the egg, right on her shoe. It broke and was a huge mess!"

I try not to laugh, but it's hard.

Mae nods. "I know. It would've been funny,

but then the worse thing happened. It's terrible."

I make myself be serious. "What worse thing?"

Mae rubs her eyes. "April snuck up on Squirrel to give him a surprise hug, and he got scared and totally freaked out. He scratched her arm. Her mom had to come early and get her. Our playdate was ruined."

I can't believe it. That *is* terrible. "Did she go to the hospital?"

Mae shakes her head. "No, but she was screaming and crying and she needed a bunch of bandages."

I don't know what to say. I want to give her my helping hand right now, except that I have no idea what to write on it.

CHAPTER

23

The bell rings just as we get to school. We go straight into class and sit down. I sneak a look across the table. April looks perfectly normal except for three small bandages on her right arm.

She's talking to Ava and being super loud. I know why. She wants everyone to hear.

"I'll probably have trouble writing today, because of my arm."

Ava nods. "You're so brave!"

"What happened?" asks Jennifer.

April makes a sad face. "Cat attack! From a *not* friendly cat." She taps her pencil on the table. "I'm rethinking my favorite pet choice."

"Rabbits!" says Jennifer. "You'll love them. They're amazing. I have one."

April nods. "They are cute. Do they scratch?"

Jennifer shakes her head. "No, never, unless they're scared or you sneak up on them. Rabbits don't like surprises."

"Humph!" April grunts. "I didn't know pets were so moody."

Steven leans forward. "MOOOOOO-DY! Well, don't get a cow then."

Everyone laughs, except April. She looks like

she might cry. Suddenly I feel a little bit bad for her, but I don't want to. She doesn't deserve my sad feelings.

When the lunch bell rings, I watch the door. April and Ava leave together. Ava puts her arm through April's and smiles super big. I wonder if Ava's happy about the disaster. Happy to have April all to herself again.

Mae sits with me at lunch. I'm glad she played tag. Now she knows everyone. Does Mae miss April? Does April miss Mae? I watch them, but it's impossible to tell. At recess we play tag again, but not with the blue owl. I left it at home.

On the way back to class, Mae shows me a pencil. "Do you think April's going to want this back? It's from her collection. It's probably special."

That's not an easy question to answer. April's brain is hard to figure out.

Mae shakes her head. "I just don't know what to do."

I put my arm around her and give her a fast hug. It's not an answer, but it makes her smile, just a little bit.

CHAPTER

24

Mae and I walk home together. We don't talk about April—instead she tells me about her brother, Rocket. He likes racing, his favorite color is orange, and he's starting a rock band. Now I know more about Isabella, too.

Mae's coming over, so we go straight to my house.

As soon as we walk in, Mae bends down and pets Sammy. "Hi, Sammy! You're the best dog!"

"Can we keep her?" asks Sammy.

I laugh.

Mae looks up. "What's so funny?"

I don't know what to say. Do I tell her about Sammy talking? What if she thinks it's weird? What if she doesn't want to be friends? But I don't have to worry, because Isabella suddenly walks in and Mae forgets about me laughing. After everyone says hi, we go up to my room. Mae can't wait to see the Wonder Wheel. I let her spin it, just for fun. There are two slices left, Poem and Dance/Spin Again.

Suddenly Sammy has an idea. "Mae can come over tomorrow and help us spin it."

That's a great idea. I look at Mae. "Will you?"

Mae's confused. "Will I what?"

Oh no! I forgot. She can't hear Sammy.

Now I *have* to tell her about him talking.

Sammy's not like me. He's not worried. My insides feel swirly and gurgly. It's not easy to talk, but I do it. After I tell her, Mae has a hundred questions. Things like, Does anyone else know? Have you always been able to talk to him? Can other people hear him? Can he talk to cats? I answer everything, and when I'm done, she tells us a story.

"I used to have a friend named Marigold. I talked to her all the time, but no one ever saw her except for me."

"I'm glad I'm not invisible," says Sammy. "How'd she eat?"

That makes me laugh, so I tell Mae, and soon we are all laughing, but I'm laughing the hardest, because Mae's still here and she believes me.

Just before bed, I hand out my helping hand.

Isabella's pretty surprised. She reads it out loud. "Wear orange to the audition."

I put my hand over my heart. "It's true. It'll help."

She nods. We never lie about hand over heart.

CHAPTER

25

Today Mae is going to help us spin the wheel.
She knocks on the door just as I'm finishing with
breakfast. I let her in and we all run straight up
to my room. Mae throws her coat onto my bed.

"Look," says Sammy. "You're twins."

Mae and I are both wearing blue shirts and
brown pants, but the rest of us is not twins. Mae
is taller than me and she has black curly hair.

Mae thinks she's just going to watch me and
Sammy, but I tell her the surprise. She's going to
spin.

"REALLY?" She jumps up and down, and then runs to the wheel and gives it a giant pull.

"WOODPECKERS!" says Sammy. "A million of them!"

We watch and watch and watch, until it stops. A million woodpeckers takes forever.

"DANCE/SPIN AGAIN!" shouts Mae. "It's the winner!"

I get the note and read it aloud.

DANCE/SPIN AGAIN

It's always fun to DANCE. Put on some music and do three minutes of silly dancing. When you're done, spin the wheel again. Have fun!

Sammy and I know exactly what kind of dancing to do — On-the-Ground Disco Dancing!

Mae is good at learning moves. By the end of the song, we can all point in different directions at the same time.

After the dancing, we spin again. This time Mae and I do it together. We're all hoping for the same thing—more dancing—but we get Poem.

"Yay! POEM!" We shout and cheer anyway.

I read the note.

FEEL-GOOD POEM

Make up a silly feel-good poem for a friend. Try to make them smile. You must use at least three of these words in your poem: pumpkin, zebra, friend, brave, famous, cactus, fantastic, surprise.

Have fun!

"What about me?" asks Mae. "Do I do it too?"

I hold up my hand. "As an official spinner, you have to."

"JUNE! SCHOOL! FAST!"

Mom is yelling at us from downstairs. I look at the clock. Mom's right. We're late. Mae grabs her coat and we race out of the room.

CHAPTER 26

We make it to class just in time. It's hard to be calm and my heart's still racing, even after I sit down.

When the lunch bell rings, Mae walks straight over to April and hands her a note. April reads it and then smiles.

Mae holds up a pencil.

April nods. "You can keep it."

"Are you sure?"

April nods again. "It's not that super special. I have three more just the same."

Ava walks over to see what's going on, but April shoves the note in her pocket, and then she and Ava walk out, arm in arm again.

"What did you give her? Is it a secret? Why was she happy?" I have lots of questions for Mae.

On the way to the lunchroom she tells me everything. "When April came to my house, she thought Rocket's band was super cool. So I told her what he did. He changed his band name to Cat Scratch Shrieker, because of her. I made it into a poem."

At first I'm jealous about the band name, but that feeling goes away when Mae tell me more.

"Rocket changes his band name a lot. It'll probably be something different next week."

At recess, I sit on the grass while Mae plays tag with Leni and Jules. I'm writing my poem. I thought it would be a poem for Mae, but when I start, it turns into something else.

Being Rabbitastic
Is fantastic
You do not want a cat
We all know that
For a dog you might cry
But why not try
A bunny like a dog
Hops like a frog
No zebra or bat
Will be all that
He can fetch, jump, and bite
A friend day and night

I'm excited about it until I get to class, and then I get worried. What if Steven thinks it's weird? But I have no choice. I have to give it to him. It's too late to make up a new one. I hand it to Jennifer and she passes it over.

Steven reads it and then smiles. "Guess what? We're getting a rabbit on Saturday."

Jennifer claps her hands. "REALLY!" She can hardly believe it. And then she and Steven talk nonstop about rabbits.

CHAPTER 27

Mae can't come over after school. She's going shopping with her mom, but we still walk home together. We talk about the Wonder Wheel. Mae is sad it's over.

I shake my head. "But it's not! On Monday we get to set up a whole new wheel, with new stuff to do all week. And then there's four more after that."

Mae and I try to guess what'll be on the new wheel, but it's impossible. All I can say is "If Grandma Penny made it, it'll be good."

When we get to Mae's house, her mom's already in the car, so I talk fast. "Come over tomorrow morning. There's a surprise."

Mae looks excited. "What kind of surprise?"

I shake my head. "I can't tell you, but bring a shovel."

Mae nods. "I have my own shovel!"

I smile. I already know that.

We wave back and forth until they turn the corner and I can't see them anymore.

I get to the house just as Isabella's leaving for her audition. She's carrying her little suitcase and her nails are painted bright orange.

"Good luck!" I lift my hand up for a high-five, but she ignores it and mumbles something I can't understand. Maybe she's too nervous for high-fives.

"YOU'RE HOME!" Sammy jumps on me the second I open the door. It's nice to feel welcome.

After playing and snacks, we go up to my room. I find my blue collection and dump everything out onto the floor.

Sammy sniffs them. "Are we looking for more blue things?"

I hold up the owl. "No, we're burying treasure."

"DIGGING!" shouts Sammy, and a second later he's racing down the stairs.

Sammy loves digging almost as much as he loves chasing squirrels. I grab a yellow marker and the plastic bag and run after him. He's at the back door, waiting to go out. Before I open it, I color the owl's eyes with the marker and wrap it up in the bag.

We bury it in the backyard. Sammy digs the hole, I drop in the bag, and then he covers it up. It's teamwork, and when we're done, we high-five. Hand to paw.

CHAPTER

28

Sammy and I wake up early. The house smells terrific!

Mom's cooking, but she's not making breakfast—she's making lemon cake. She lets me clean the spoon. Mae rings the doorbell right at my last lick.

She holds up her shovel, then sniffs. "What smells so good?"

"Lemon cake!" I show her the little window on the oven and point to the one for her family.

She licks her lips. "I wish I could eat it now."

I know exactly how she feels.

"CAN WE DO IT? CAN WE?" Sammy doesn't care about lemon cake. He wants to go outside. I open the door and we follow him to the digging spot.

The hole isn't deep. Mae finds the plastic bag after only a few scoops. She opens it and gasps. "It's your owl, but with yellow eyes! Like my lucky bird! Really? You made it for me?"

"Thank you!" She holds it tight and then gives me a hug. Sammy's too busy for hugs. He's filling up the hole.

Isabella pokes her head out the upstairs

window and yells at us. "Mom says to stop digging holes in the yard."

"What hole?" I point to the ground. Sammy's a professional. The hole's gone.

Mae waves hi at Isabella. "Rocket said you're in the band and that you're good!"

Isabella doesn't say anything, but I can guess why. She's probably rolling her eyes. She waves back and shuts the window.

Mae stares at the window for an extra second, then looks at me. "Guess what?"

"Dinosaur bones!" says Sammy.

I shrug. "Unicorns?"

Mae claps. "No better."

"Better than unicorns?" I shake my head. That's impossible.

"It's a secret," says Mae. We lean in to hear.

She points up at Isabella's window. "If we got

your sister to marry my brother, you and I would be sisters."

It's a great idea, but there's a problem. "Isabella's not allowed to have a boyfriend yet."

Mae smiles. "That's okay, we can make it happen later. Like in ten years."

Now I'm smiling too. A friend for ten years just might be better than unicorns.